APOLLO
AMBITION

BY

MARTIN KIELTY

WITH ILLUSTRATIONS BY

JIM MacNEE

ISBN 978-1-326-48380-7

SENNACHIE
PRESS

www.sennachie-press.co.uk

FOREWORD

I miss the Apollo, and that's why I wrote this story.

Apollo Memories, my book that includes real accounts of real
nights at the Purple Palace, was first published in 2005.
It's never been out of print since. Every now and again I get
to talk about those incredible adventures in a magazine article,
a radio interview or a TV show, and it never gets old.

Scott McArthur and Andy Muir's **GlasgowApollo.com** website
started it all. In recent years there have been several other ways to
celebrate the old Green's Playhouse, notably Tommy McGrory's
work with the Loud And Proud Orchestra's *I Was There* musical
(now rewritten, and to be staged again in 2016).

I wanted a way of taking another wee wander down memory lane,
by describing for posterity an average night in the venue – even
though we all know there was no such thing. So while Logie
McFarlane, Wheech McGhee, Night Garden and other characters
are purely fictional, I haven't strayed far from things that either
did happen, or at least *could* have happened.

Thanks to Jim MacNee for livening up the story with some
beautifully-observed illustrations that I know will colour up your
own wee wander.

*Dedicated to the Glasgow choir, who are a part
of world cultural history and can never be forgotten.*

MK, November 2015

MONDAY, MAY 1, 1978

THE SMELL OF BLAW rose from the basement at Listen Records. That was normal. What wasn't normal was the presence of Wheech McGhee, who should have been at work. Logie McFarlane went down the stairs and took his time to admire the photos from the AC/DC show the previous night, which displayed Bon, Angus and the boys in their full glory. There was the guitarist on the singer's shoulders, there was the bouncer glaring furiously as he kept an eye on Angus as he played guitar from one of the boxes, and there was the band, lined up in Scotland shirts, saluting the Glasgow choir.

"Brilliant night," Wheech said from his position against the counter, scratching the growth on his fascinatingly askew face. "Ah'm still buzzin'."

"Whit are you daein oot?" Logie asked.

"May Day holiday, innit?"

"No' for you – you work for the cooncil. Or at least ye'r *paid* by the cooncil. You're aff *next* Monday, no' this."

Wheech shrugged. "Ah'll say ah got confused," he said. "It's in the paper – some folk oan, some folk aff, naebody knows whit's whit. And ah'm still buzzin' anyway. Ah'd dae nothin' at the depot."

"You dae nothin' anyway. Great pictures, in't they?"

"Ah wuz there," said Danny, the tall, thin hippie behind the counter, responsible for most of the smell.

"Who wuzny?" Wheech demanded. He held up the rolled-back sleeves of his patched denim jacket to show that he'd scrawled "AC" on one and "DC" on the other, then slammed his fists together to join the letters up. "World's greatest rock an' roll band. Fi' Cranhill an'aw."

Logie stared closely at one of the pictures. "Ye can just see me in that yin," he grinned. "Can ye buy it yet?"

"No' yet," Danny told him. "The boy's getting them printed later. Want ti place an order?"

"Nae bother. How does he dae it?"

"What, get a camera intae the Apollo?"

"It's Green's, ya prick," Wheech glared.

Danny ignored him. "Naebody knows. He'll no' tell. All we know is, he gets by the bouncers every time, then brings the photies in here." He coughed, and reached for a small tin box under the counter. "Public service, if ye ask me."

"Roll me wan," Wheech said, nodding towards the tin.

"Dae wan," Danny replied briskly, laying his makings out

in front of him.

Logie continued staring at the picture. It brought it all back – four thousand frantic fans, maybe more, in the stinking old venue they called home. The Apollo, the Purple Palace, still Green's Playhouse to some: a converted cinema with a dangerously high and dangerously sloping stage, at eye level with a balcony that bounced to the beat of the best bands in the world. He reached out towards the photo, stroking the air in front as if to feel that feeling all over again.

Heartbreaking to believe it would soon be over for ever.

A lanky, dark-haired character nearly fell down the stairs over his own long legs as he galloped towards the counter, forcing Logie out of his dream state as he was pushed out the way. "Is it here? Ye said Monday," he said.

"Calm yer jets, Varicose – it's here, it's here," Danny told him, waving both hands in a downward direction, a massive spliff between the fingers of his right (which Wheech was staring at intently).

"Can ah huv it?" Varicose spluttered, forcing his hand into a tight jeans pocket, spilling more money on the floor than he managed to keep in his grasp.

Danny took a big draw. "Aye," he breathed back heavily. "In a minute."

"Whit can he huv?" Wheech asked, his face dotting round in the air in an attempt to catch as much blaw whiff as he could.

The hippie put the joint in his mouth and leaned over to

open a box, then stood up again, holding an LP like it was a religious artifact. "This," he said through another puff.

"Rainbow," Varicose whispered. "*Long Live Rock And Roll. No oot yet. Ya fuckin' dancer.*" He held out his money, and, exchange secured, stared at the album cover like a long-lost love. The iconic line-drawings of the five band members and the archaic lettering did give an impression of religion – although Varicose was well overdoing it.

"Here, that's no' what ye telt *me* it wid cost!" Wheech said.

Danny gave him a dismissive look. "Varicose spends mair than anyone else on imports. He gets discounts. You don't. Coz *you* are a wee fanny."

"I'd buy mair if ah hud mair ti spend," Wheech grumbled, stuffing his hands into his pockets.

"Ye'd have mair ti spend if ye didn't keep getting yer pay docked for doggin' it," Logie told him as he came up to the counter and shoved his friend's shoulder. "By the way, huv ye got money the day? Ye'v to get the Thin Lizzy ticket."

"Course ah huv! Ye want ti go up the noo?"

"Might as well." Logie looked at his watch. "Time ti get the ticket, get a few pints in then go back fur the show."

"Night Gerden?" Danny laughed. "Ye'r no going to see that pish, ur ye?"

"Shut it," Logie told him.

"Ye'd be as well savin' yer money for a band that plays music," the hippie went on. "Ye'v got Jethro Tull, Sabbath,

Lizzy, UFO comin' up..."

"Don McLean, Ian Dury, Bowie," Varicose added.

"Ah'm goin' ti Sabbath, Lizzy, UFO and Bowie, and maybe mair," Logie replied. "But Night Gerden will dae fur me. Proper good rock'n'roll, they are. Ye were at AC/DC – if ye huv the sense ti' like them ye'll like Night Gerden an'aw."

Danny shook his head. "Not any more, pal," he said. "Ye know they've gone punk?"

"Yer arse!" Logie spat back.

"Ah'm no kiddin' ye," Danny said, waving his joint in the air. "Said it in the *NME*."

"Who reads that pish?" Wheech laughed, although Varicose, finally waking up from his experience with the Rainbow album, nodded in agreement with Danny.

"Plenty o'folk," the hippie said. "An' anyway – ah'v heard

the single."

"Talk shite," Logie said threateningly.

"And it's a *punk* single."

"Fuck up!" Logie bellowed. "Let me hear it then!"

"Canny dae that – no' oot yet," Danny shrugged. "But ye'll find oot soon enough. They'll probably play it tonight." He leaned over the counter. "And I'll tell ye whit. It's pish. They'll no' be playin' the Apollo again if that's the pish they're gonny come oot wi'."

"*Naebody* will be playin' the Apollo again, efter July," Varicose said, forcing a silence upon the room.

They didn't want to think about it. The venue closing? It was more than unfair. It was brutal. It was like being up the Royal Infirmary, waiting for your old uncle to die, or something. And to be told that the music was going to stop so that the building could become a bingo hall, of all things...

Wheech shook his head. "Mon," he said. "I need a pint noo."

Logie looked at the picture one more time. "Mind an' get me wan o'them," he told Danny as he followed Wheech up the stairs.

"Nae bother," the hippie replied after him, feeling bad about where he'd taken the conversation. Varicose stared deeply into the Rainbow record as the blaw smoke settled into a slow dance round the record shelves.

"HOW MANY FOOTSTEPS is it again?" Logie asked, stopping his mate in his tracks at the Listen door.

"Six hunner an' therty-four," Wheech said.

They counted as they made their way up Renfield Street. It was a good way of avoiding the kind of talk that might come after what had been said in the shop. And despite everything, Danny knew his music. So if he said Night Garden had abandoned their heavy rock sound (like so many other bands were trying to do right now) in a bid to jump onto the punk rock gravy train — but it didn't bear thinking about.

Not that there was much wrong with punk. It had its moments, and plenty of them. Logie's band played straight no-nonsense rock, with attention to melody, delivery and construction. But there was no denying a certain amount of attraction in something a little bit less restrained.

He'd slightly modified the standard hair-and-denim look to include some sharp cutting around his sideburns and a modern cut to his clothes, replacing the loose threads with a tighter fit that had a suggestion of military about it.

But that didn't mean he wanted his idols to do the same.

Night Garden weren't the size of AC/DC, Led Zeppelin, Black Sabbath, Status Quo or any of those bands. They hadn't had the breaks, maybe, or there's just a chance they didn't have the songs. But they *did* have the feel, the groove, the attitude, and a real rocking honesty about them.

There might have been a punk spirit about them – there was a punk spirit about almost any band that ever mattered

– but that didn't make them a punk band. They played complex chords, they played lead solos, and aye, okay, there was even the odd drum solo. But what was so wrong with that?

If the hundreds of world-class bands who'd played the Apollo had taught the average Glasgow gig-goer one thing, it

was that there was room for all forms of music, ABBA to Zappa. If you really listened you could get something out of anything. If you did your bit as a member of the audience, you could learn something. Almost every band in the world had at least one song worth hearing – even those shit support acts who got booed off, probably.

Night Garden had nothing to be ashamed of. It worried Logie that *he* was sure of that, while the band themselves might not be. It suggested there was nothing to grip onto, nothing that stood still, nothing you could rely on from the moment you were born until the moment you died.

That's how important music was. That's how important the

Apollo was. That's how important Night Garden not being punk was.

"Eight hunner and twenty-eight," Wheech said.

Logie hadn't even noticed as they'd approached 126 Renfield Street, arrived under the overhang and passed Mr Chips. Now they were standing in front of the three double doors, three steps to the one on the right, two to the middle and one to the left, the space-age "Apollo" sign above and the display boards to either side reading: "*Live on stage: Night Garden In Concert, Mon 1 May 7 30.*"

"It's six hunner and therty-four if ye get green men aw' the way up. An' if ye don't huv ti go ti West Nile Street fur a cerry-oot."

"Whit? Oh – aye," Logie said. "Let's get in. It's freezin' the day."

The gloomy purple foyer was busier than might be expected for a Monday. The bank holiday was a more likely explanation than the board listing the tickets that had just gone on sale. It looked like everything up to and including the Last Show was available: Tull, Don McLean, Sabbath with someone called Van Halen, the Darts, the Stranglers with the Skids, Ian Dury and the Blockheads, the Buzzcocks, Thin Lizzy with Johnny Cougar, four nights of Bowie, the Boomtown Rats, UFO, the Clash with Suicide and the Specials... and Christian leading what was promised to be a gala closing event – complete with the venue's only-ever license to sell alcohol.

"Logie, ya prick! Comin' to the show the night?" a heavily-bearded fat cheery character wandered up.

"Course ah'm ur, Tam," Logie replied. "How's Rab McGillis doin'?"

"Stupit arsehole," Tam said. "He got oot last night. Nothin' too serious. Second-degree burns an'that, know?"

Wheech laughed. "Noo that wuz funny! Mind, ah telt him no' ti dae it."

"You gied him the lighter!" Tam said, eyebrows high.

"Aye, an' ah put the carpet roon him ti' put him oot!"

"Settin' himself on fire. What a prick!"

"Worked, though," Wheech said. "Got us in the papers." He pulled out a torn-out page from the morning edition. "*Guitarist sets fire to himself at pop concert*," he read.

"*Thousands of fans at a pop concert at the Kelvingrove bandstand, Glasgow, watched as a member of one of the bands set fire to himself on stage.*

"*Robert McGillis, 21, poured methylated spirits on his clothes then set himself alight. Other musicians rushed to his aid and wrapped him in a carpet to smother the flames.*"

"That's wrang," Wheech interrupted himself, waving a finger in the air. "It wuzny any o' yous, it was *me* – it was a roadie who saved him, no' a musician."

He continued: "*Concert organisers said they had no idea why McGillis would set fire to himself, but that he had been suffering from depression. A band member added: 'I think it was a cry for help.'*

"The free concert was staged to draw attention to plans to close down the Apollo. McGillis' band was one of seven to take part, including Glasgow rising-stars Fox Ache."

"See – got us a mention!" Wheech said to Logie. "Fame at last!"

"Cry for help?" Logie said, ignoring the compliment because it meant nothing to him. "I've seen McGillis do that a hunner times. He was meant ti put the meths jist on the bottom o' his jeans. But he was pished and got it aw' doon his legs."

"He says he's gonny do it next time an'aw," Tam laughed. "If he's got a band, that is."

"Amazin', the things ye'll come up wi ti hide the fact ye canny play," Wheech reflected. He held up his plastic bag of beer tins, purchased on the way up the hill. "I'm away ti stash these. Want ti get the Lizzy ticket?"

"Want ti gie us the money?" Logie said pointedly, hand forcefully held out until his mate grudgingly laid out two pound notes. "It's *three* quid." An even-more grudged final pound appeared, before Wheech turned his back and slid suspiciously through the doors that led into the venue.

"Yous were brilliant yesterday," Tam said. "What are yes gonny do next? Ye canny just play the Howff an'that every week – yous are better than that."

"We're talkin' aboot it," Logie reassured him. "But it's no that simple. Some of the boys have got commitments, know? I wuz thinking we need ti go ti London or somethin'."

"London? Och, can ye no' get a record deal here?"

"We're no' a punk band," Logie said. "Naebody in Glesga's signing anybody, and ye'll only get a deal in Embra if ye'r a punk band."

"Could you no' jist, like, become a punk band? Fox Ache is still a brilliant name fur a punk band."

Logie looked at him. He didn't mean any harm. It was a simple question from a fan who just wanted to see his band do well. Nothing wrong with that. If anything, the band owed their fans some success to bask in. Never mind the struggle to keep the group together. Never mind the number of times someone couldn't be arsed learning their part, or didn't turn up for rehearsal, or turned up late, without gear, without their share of whatever it cost to do whatever it was. Never mind the attempt to rewrite a word or two of a song in the hope of getting a bigger cut of publishing money that probably would never come. Never mind the dirge of loading in, setting up, sound-checking, waiting, waiting, waiting, for an hour of sheer energetic joy – soon to be forgotten in the rush to break down, load out and get home, then go to work the next day.

Never mind. "Maybe," Logie said, moving away from Tam. "We'll make it happen – don't worry about that." *He* did, though.

The booking office area was miraculously empty, meaning he didn't have to make his way through hordes of hopefuls wanting to know when Quo, Rush, Alex Harvey or whatever else tickets went on sale. Because, of course, the answer would be "never."

With AC/DC's departure a few hours ago, almost all the

bands that truly connected with the deep beating heart of the Apollo – who really got it, really dug it, really *really* felt it and meant it – had already played their last show there. The exceptions were Thin Lizzy, and probably the Stranglers.

Logie gently tapped the window and leaned down towards the circular opening. "Awright, Sharon?"

The girl behind the counter looked up from the TV listings in the paper, her usual unimpressed expression dropped as soon as she realised who she was talking to. "Logie – hullo! Ye awright?"

"Aye, hen. Jist efter a Thin Lizzy ticket. Stalls."

"Jist the wan?" she grinned, running her hand through her hair.

"Aye. Ah'll meet mah mates inside."

"So ye will," she laughed. "Ah seen ye at Kelvingrove yesterday – ye were brilliant. Ah wuz in the crowd gettin' signatures for the petition."

"That's brilliant. Many did ye get?"

"Hunners," she shrugged. "That cooncillor says there's mair than forty thousand on it noo. They canny close the Apollo wi' forty thousand folk telling them ti keep it, can they?"

"Ah don't know..." Logie said.

"*He* says they canny." Her face lit up. "Here, were ye at the show last night?"

"Course I wuz!" Logie frowned. "Where else wid ah be?"

"Might huv been playin' yer ain gig. Ye know ma pal Carol? She went ti a party wi Bon Scott. In Drumchapel!"

"Yer arse!"

"She did! One o'wur pals got backstage and he was talkin' ti Bon and says he hud an empty. He says, 'D'ye want ti come back?' So Bon got a cerry-oot and went back ti Drumchapel – and Carol winched him."

"Aye?"

"Aye! Coulda gone further an'aw," Sharon said with a leer. "But ma pal's ma and da came back early an' they aw hud ti dae a runner. She dreeped aff the back wall wi' Bon!"

"Brilliant!" Logie grinned, deciding not to display his doubt.

The clark looked down at her paper. "See who's on *Whistle Test* themorra? Todd Rundgren, Paul Butterfield and Doctor John. No bad, eh?"

"Haw, bigyin!" came a voice from his left, where a queue had formed while Sharon spoke. "Gonny get yer ticket and get yer arse oot the way?"

"Shurrit!" said another. "That's Logie McFarlane fi Fox Ache!"

"I don't gie a fuck if it's John Greig. He can move his arse."

Logie put Wheech's three pounds through the gap at the bottom of the window, and Sharon pushed a ticket back in return, along with a sheet of paper and a pen. "Sign the petition," she said.

"Already huv," he said.

"Dae it again!" she replied, pushing two more pens through. "Three different names, three different inks."

"'Mon, big man!" said someone in the queue.

"He's signing the Apollo petition!" said another.

"Aye, well..."

Logie scribbled down three alternate entries. "Ah've no hud the chance ti play here yet. It canny close till then, eh?"

"It's no' gonny close," Sharon said forcefully. "Forty thousand signatures. Paul McCartney, Eric Clapton and Robert Plant huv signed it. McCartney and Clapton really *huv* signed it!"

Logie grinned. "An' there's your job an'aw," he said.

"Ah'll be awright," she replied, fixing her hair and grinning. "Ah'm thinkin' o' becomin' a model. Folk say ah look like Karen Flynn aff the Tennent's cans!"

"Ye dae that, hen," Logie replied, considering that there was half a chance it might be nearly true, in the right light, with the right amount of lager put away. "See ye later."

"POVERTY CORNER, THEN?" Wheech asked as they left the gloom of the foyer for a bright but cold Renfield Street. "Or Boots Corner?"

"Poverty Corner," Logie said. "Ah'm wantin' a pint."

"Ah'm no botherin' wi' a lumber anyway," Wheech said. "Did ye see that pure heifer ah pulled at Boots Corner the other night? Nae wonder she'd been stood up. She looked like she'd been dookin' fur chips." he sniffed. "Fun, but. She hud an empty. It wuzny empty when I wuz finished."

They crossed the road to Lauders Bar, known as Poverty Corner after the out-of-work actors who used to drink there in the hope of picking up work at the Pavillion Theatre next door. Two pints of heavy were ordered and delivered, and Logie demonstrated by his stance that he wanted to remain at the bar, rather than sit down as usual.

"What's up wi' ye, pal?" Wheech asked gently.

"Ah'm fine."

"Aye, so ye ur. An' the Sex Pistols are gettin' back thegether." In the lack of any answer he just went on talking. "So ah'm no' goin' ti Argentina efter aw. Ah'd been savin' up, like, but that wuz when it was eight hunner poon. Noo it's mair like fifteen hunner. An' that dizny count yer drinkin' money. Ah don't know how much a bevvy is in Argentina.

"Fair like their fitba' there, right enough. Did ye hear this mob o' fans went ti lynch a ref fur a dodgy penalty call? Hud him up on a rope before the polis stopped them."

He drank a large mouthful of heavy. "So ah'm just gonny get a big telly," he went on. "No' rentin' it, buyin' it. Twenty-two inch colour job for two hunner an' fifty quid, doon fi' two-eight-five. An' they're throwin' in wan o' they TV games, and that's worth fifteen quid right aff. Ah'll probably sell it – they things are shite. Stupid wee dial an' a white square oan yer screen."

Logie sighed, although not because of the banter. It was time to say it out loud for the first time. He stared through his pint glass into the bar top as he spoke. "Ah think... ah'm goin' ti leave the band."

"Aw, is that aw?" It sounded like Wheech was serious, until, after another sup of heavy, he added: "Nothing major, then. *Leave the band?* After aw' we've done wi it? After aw' *you've* done wi it?"

"Ach, it's jist... Ah don't know where it goes next. Ah don't know whit they want fi' it. Mick's got a good job wi' prospects, Tommy's huvin' a wean, an' Hendo –"

"Hendo's a wank," Wheech finished. "A wank wi' a transit van, but a wank aw' the same."

Logie remained silent for a while. "See that Kelvingrove gig? Ah wuz watchin' the other bands..."

"Ye don't want ti dae that."

"There's a shitload o' talent in the toon. Some really good people, ye know? Every bit as good as the boys who've made it oot o' here. Guitarists like Jimmy McCulloch. Bassists like Jimmy Dewar. Singers like –"

"You."

Logie shook his head. "Ah wuz watchin' these wee bands, wee like us, and ah wuz thinkin', 'There's an immense fuckin' powerhouse o' a band between some o' us'."

Wheech watched his friend's face intently. "So what are ye gonny dae?"

"Ah don't know. Ah don't know. But somethin's got ti change. Somethin' big, and for ever. Ye don't get many chances in life, know? An' ye don't get *any* if ye'r no oot there tryin' ti make them happen."

"How about playin' somewhere new? There's that place that's jist opened at Pertick Cross. Cinders. Change is as good as, innit?"

"Huv ye seen who they've got oan? Chou Pahrot an' Simple Minds. Think they want a band like us? What we're daein'… it's oot o' fashion, so it is. Naebody wants good songs wi' good lyrics. They want… Chou Pahrot an' Simple Minds."

"Here!" Wheech replied. "Don't talk pish! You saw the Green's last night – whit wuz it, six thoosand boys there fur AC/DC? Sold oot, an' then some. An' they recorded it fur an album an'aw. Ye canny tell me that's oot o' fashion."

Logie sighed again. "Ah don't know," he repeated. "Aw ah know is, there's a great big lump o' fuck-aw' happenin' right noo. An' ah'm running oot o' time to dae make somethin' happen."

He took a long drink. "Ye know… ah always thought ah'd get ti' play the Apollo. Ever since the first time ah wuz in there, ah wuz lookin' up at that stupit high stage, gaun, 'That'll be me wan day.' Well, it'll no be me, will it? Coz the whole thing's away soon.

"How do ye deal wi' that, Wheech?" he asked, staring into his mate's face. "How do ye get over the fact that, this big thing, this big ambition, has been taken oot yer hauns and punted oot the perk?"

"Ah thought yer da wuz yer influence..." Wheech muttered.

"Aye, course he is. Started me singin' and playin' dead young. An' he's still oot there daein his folk music, maist every night. But that's *different*. That'll always be there."

His tone turned almost threatening. "Mah music's gettin' punted and mah venue's gettin' punted. Whit di ah dae aboot that? *Whit the fuck di ah dae?*"

Wheen gestured for him to calm down. "Ah don't know," he admitted. "But if anyone can dae it, you can."

"Can ah?" He paused again. "All ah can dae is try."

He trailed off, his eyes flickering as if a thousand ideas were passing through his mind, even though he couldn't catch any of them. Wheech drank more of his pint and looked round the bar, so as to give his mate some space. "Name o' fuck!" he whispered.

"Whit?" Logie replied, sensing something had changed.

"Over in the corner there. It's only Davie fi' Night Gerden!"

They both stared over to a table at the window where two men were seated. There was always an aura surrounding someone in a band – more obvious when they were with the rest of the band, but present nonetheless when they weren't. Something to do with what you'd learned about people when you were forced to meet thousands of them, just because you happened to be a musician. Dave Mitchell, guitarist with Night Garden, was one such person.

"Mon over," Wheech said.

"Lie'im alane," Logie protested doubtfully.

"*Mon!*" Wheech repeated, and, noting the drinks on the table, ordered the same again, then led the way across the bar room. "Can ah get ye a drink, Dave?" he grinned, slamming two pints of lager down. "An' wan fur yer mate."

Mitchell looked up, surprised mid-sentence. "Well... thanks!" he said, his broad London accent taking a moment to be understood. "Are you coming to the show?"

"Fuckin' right!" Wheech took the guitarist's hand and shook it vigorously. "We saw ye last year an'aw. An' the year before. We've got aw yer albums, so we huv. Huven't we, Logie? This is Logie, an ah'm Wheech McGhee."

"Wheech McGhee?" Mitchell laughed at his own inability to pronounce the name, while recovering his hand. "Well, thanks!" he repeated.

"It's nice to meet ye," Logie said, deliberately slowing and lowering his voice, taking some of the edge off it for the Londoner. "We'll be in the stalls, cheering along. I hope you have a good gig."

"Logie's a singer," Wheech grinned. "Fox Ache, the best band in Glesga. You should get them oot on the next tour wi' ye! They'd sell oot the Apollo on their ain, so they wid. Easy money for ye!"

Mitchell had heard it all before so he changed the subject. "They say the Apollo's closing in July. That's a shame. You know the best thing about it for us? If play your music to the Glasgow crowd, they'll tell you what's good and what's bad. Then you change your set based on how it went down here.

"Everyone else gets a better show because of you guys. You're important. I hope that'll continue... somehow."

"Bastart city cooncil," Wheech said. "Ye canny make a profit fi' a venue wi'oot a drinks licence, and they'll no' gie wan ti the Apollo. They say the fans wid kick aff if we're pished. But what aboot fitba' fans? See the way they act on the way back fi' Hampden? An' besides, we usually *ur* pished anyway!"

Logie could tell the conversation needed to end, and that Mitchell's companion, presumably a roadie, was preparing to end it in whatever way possible. "Anyway, have a good one," he smiled, moving away and pulling on Wheech's arm.

"Best singer in Glesga," his companion whispered at the guitarist. "He's goat the anger, he's goat the attitude. You should hear how he does *Doonward Spiral*! Fuckin' amazin', so it is. Better than – well, as good as yours. Mind the name: Logie McFarlane, Fox Ache."

Mitchell grinned then returned to his conversation. Back at the bar Wheech groaned. "I never goat his fuckin' autograph!"

"Leave it," Logie told him. "Whatever they're talkin' aboot, it's important."

His friend looked longingly across the room, but realised

there was no way to force himself back into Mitchell's attention, and decided to change the subject instead. "Legs And Co are opening the DIY shop in Baillieston on Saturday," he said. "Ah'm no' missin' that!"

"GET YER TROUSERS ON – ye'r nicked," drawled a man who'd seen *Sweeney 2* twice in the past week, even though it wasn't as good as the series.

"He says if I don't sell it, he'll gie it away!" complained a teenager, whose dad refused to let him go to the Stranglers show for fear of him becoming a glue-sniffer.

"Alan Rough? Shite! There's nae way he'll no' take Jim Stewart, nae way," argued a Kilmarnock fan as he discussed Ally MacLeod's World Cup squad.

But towards the front of the queue that snaked round the Apollo, the conversation was focused on the rumours that Night Garden were about to split up.

"They're sayin' Dave Mitchell and Bobby Rycott have fell oot," a voice of authority reported loudly. "Mitch wants ti go punk and Bobby's no' huvin' it."

"Pish!"

"Wait till ye hear the single, then. Mah brother's in London an' he's heard it. Says it's pure punk, nae messin' aboot. Nae solo, nae change o'beat, just straight ahead punk."

"What's it called, if he's heard it?"

"Canny mind. Somethin' aboot jumping, ah think. But the B-side's a punked-up version o' *Doonward Spiral*, aff the first album."

"Ye canny punk that up. It's a real song!"

"Ye can punk up *any'hin'*– aw ye need is the attitude."

"Aye, and ti forget how ti play yer instrument."

"Don't gie us yer shite. How is *No More Heroes* no' a real song?"

"Easy – coz it isnae punk."

"You jist canny stop talkin' shite, can ye?"

Logie stood among the crowd of strangers, united by the upcoming concert and a mutual affection for its location, and watched the argument bounce around. He hadn't heard the single, but he'd watched Mitchell's behaviour in Lauders for over an hour, and the guitarist had the air of someone who'd made a decision and intended to stick with it.

But worse, *Downward Spiral* was one of his favourite Night Garden songs – actually one of his favourite songs altogether, and he felt a genuine chill of concern as he considered the possibility of a punk version.

Not that it would have to be terrible. A good song is a good song, is what conventional wisdom says. A set of chords, lyrics and a melody, and everything after that is arrangement, and arrangements can and do change. If someone played a song on the Apollo stage the way it had been played on the record, people felt let down. That's why live albums were so popular – you got to hear the songs in a different arrangement, in a different environment. The music came to life.

So if *Downward Spiral*, a number that was definitely one of Night Garden's angriest, could be done as a punk song (and it most definitely could), why shouldn't Night Garden themselves do it? But still...

A cheer came up as the doors were opened, and the queue quickly began to move. Logie was hauf-cut but not pished, unlike the bloke further ahead who couldn't stop singing and was never going to be allowed in, despite his pals' attempts to make him shut up. They made it into the foyer, but the worst was yet to come.

"Tickets ready!" bellowed a voice with a nasty tinge. Malky, one of the senior bouncers, in size as well as position, prowled across the entrance way to the main auditorium, with four of his accomplices waiting nearby, ready to pounce with the slightest excuse, their tuxedos and bow ties some kind of terrible physical joke.

Plenty of people let out a sigh of resentment when they heard Malky. "Nae ticket, nae teeth!" It always seemed as if he thought he was being funny when he said that, when in fact there was more than a little truth to it.

The drunk guy wouldn't stop singing AC/DC's *The Jack*, so his mates had concluded the only way to get him in was to sing along with him. "Shut the fuck up!" Malky screamed at them – and even the drunk guy did so.

Logie thought he was going to pass into the hall unhindered

for once, until he felt the giant hand clamp down on his neck. "Whit are you daein here, McFarlane, ya we smartass?" Malky demanded, twisting him round until their faces were inches apart.

"Come on, Malky – Night Gerden are one o' mah favourite bands. You know that!"

"They're wan o' *mah* favourite bands," said the bouncer. "Miles better than your lot. Ah saw ye at Kelvingrove. Ye were shite."

"Just tryin' ti keep the place open, Malky."

"Aye, well..." It was difficult to imagine where else in the world an Apollo bouncer could find a job that let him behave the way he could in the venue (they were unlikely to enjoy a career as a bingo caller) so the thought even put a lid on their aggressive tendencies. "On yer ain, ur ye?"

Before he could answer, a young man to their right was discovered trying to sneak in a carry-out. With a roar of fury two bouncers jumped on him and he disappeared in a cloud of torn plastic bag and lager tins. Logie tried to take the chance to slip away, but instead found himself lifted into the air with one hand around his neck, while Malky watched the unfortunate punter knocked about then kicked out. Everyone else just tried to get into the venue without falling victim.

"Noo, where were we?" Malky turned back, glaring at Logie and ignoring the fact that he was making it difficult for the smaller man to breathe. "Aye, so, ye think ye'r a Night Gerden fan?"

"Aye..."

"Well, huv ye got their new single?"

"No oot. It's no oot..."

"How come *ah've* got it, then?" The bouncer leered as he felt inside his jacket and produced the seven-inch vinyl record. The cover clearly read *"Night Garden"* and *"Jump C/W Downward Spiral (New Version)"* while four ink scrawls demonstrated that Malky had also met the band and had his copy autographed.

"How did ye get that?"

"Ah kicked it oot o'someone," Malky laughed. "Actually, the band gave it to me," he said. "And signed it 'To Malky' – huv *you* got anyhin' like that?"

"Naw..."

"Well ye'r no' a fan, then, ur ye? Go on, away in an' learn somethin'." He dropped Logie, who did his best to act as if he hadn't been nearly suffocated. "Mebbe you'll realise yer band is shite, and give it up. Ye'v nae talent, McFarlane. Jist like yer da."

Logie didn't rise to it. Instead he hurried through the doors and made his way up the flights of stairs to the busy gents' toilets. One of the advantages of being treated badly by the bouncers was that they were less likely to check your ticket, making the next step of the evening easier, as he waited his turn to reach the window.

Outside in Renfrew Lane, Wheech waited in a small crowd,

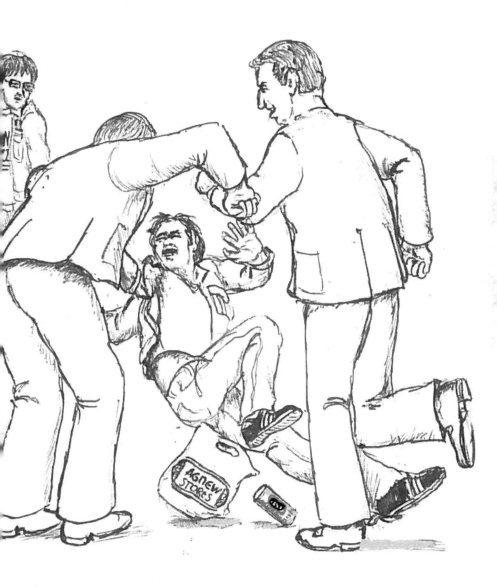

hands in pockets, eyes upward towards the toilet window. A stone was thrown out and down, landing on the ground just behind the people who waited. One of them recovered it, removed the rubber band around it, unfolded the ticket and said: "RW?"

"That's me," said another, taking it and walking off.

Soon two matchboxes fell to the roadway, one marked "L McF," which Wheech announced was his. He opened the box, retrieved Logie's ticket and marched briskly along the lane, turned right, passed Mr Chips once again and entered the Apollo foyer. With the crowd having dwindled the staff took more time to check tickets, and the tearing of the stub meant Logie's couldn't be used again. But twice was enough, and Wheech had bought a Thin Lizzy ticket to return the favour.

The scruffy one made his own way to the toilets, now empty, where Logie was waiting. "Ye no' got it yet?" Wheech asked.

"Engaged," Logie replied, nodding towards the shut cubicle half-way along the row.

"Aw this time?" Wheech muttered, and banged the door. "Here, you! Are ye awright? Get oot o'there!" A muffled reply made no sense. "Move, or ah'll kick it in!" He turned and whispered, "He'll think it's a bouncer." Then, "*Move!*" he repeated. "Och, fuck this!"

Like the rest of the venue, it didn't take much to knock over, pull down or otherwise break, and the door was thrown open. Inside, a horrified punter with long brown hair, an oversized coat and baggy trousers sat on the toilet, clothes fully on, desperately trying to hide two cameras with giant lenses.

"You're the photographer!" Wheech said. "Brilliant!"

"Thought ye were a bouncer," gasped the other. "Don't dae that again!"

"Sorry, sorry. But mah cerry-oot's in there."

"If ye'd just said that..."

"Here, ah luv yer photies. You dae the wans in Listen?"

"Aye, but don't tell embdy."

"Ye'r awright, ah'll no'. And he'll no' either."

"Logie fi Fox Ache?" said the photographer. "Ah've wanted to take pictures o'ye fur ages. Missed ye at Kelvingrove. Where are ye playin' next?"

Logie shrugged. "Probably the Howff. Again."

The noise of violence from the corridor warned them it was no time for idle chat. The photographer slid his cameras into his coat pockets and slid out of the room, while Wheech closed the cubicle door and Logie pretended to be using the urinal. Heavy footsteps and a forced-open door announced the arrival of a bouncer, who, on seeing the place was more or less bereft of potential victims, turned away again, saying with heavy sarcasm: "Enjoy yer pish, sir..."

Wheech stood up on the toilet seat and forced one of the ceiling panels up and out of its position, moving it to one side, recovering his bag of beer tins, then replacing it. He appeared out of the cubicle as if he'd only been attending a call of nature. "Right, let's get pished," he said.

TO SOME PEOPLE it was the stink of stale sweat and other bodily fluids. To others it was the magical aroma of energy and passion – even the sticky kind. But there was no mistaking the scent in the Apollo auditorium. It was held tight in damp carpets, dyed purple but with the phrase "It's Good It's Green's" still visible from the old days, and on moist plaster-work that took any opportunity to cover your clothes and hair in poorly-glued glitter. If you'd been to a show in the Purple Palace there was no denying it until you'd had a good wash.

The lights were down and the atmosphere was thicker than the smell. Silhouettes moved everywhere, catching the odd point of light here, blocking out another there, waving, shout-ing, laughing – while marauding torches provided people with enough notice to stop doing whatever they were doing before a bouncer made them.

The room was nearly full because people expected their money's worth, even if they didn't know anything about the support band. On the sloping stage, three times the height of the punters, four beleaguered characters were doing their best to make an impression upon the Glasgow choir, not many of whom were making it easy.

A thin blond Englishman, fronting the band, made the

mistake of showing he'd lost his bottle as his voice broke while he said: "This next song —"

"Is shite!" shouted someone in the stalls.

"And it better be yer last!" called another, while the row of bouncers below the stage glared around in the hope of administering a kicking.

The singer abandoned his plans to get the crowd on side by talking, counted to four and shut his eyes. It would soon be over.

"Who the fuck are they anyway?" Wheech said, lowering his beer tin as a bouncer passed in the gangway, and pushing himself tight against Logie to make it look less like they were both hovering on the same seat.

"The Fit-Ups," Logie told him, examining a flier he'd picked up from the seat.

"The Fit-Ups? The Fuck-Ups, mair like," Wheech said, starting in reply then shouting his chosen name. "Shut up, Fuck-Ups!" He grabbed the flier, quickly folded it into a paper plane, and threw it towards the stage.

"Haw – that coupon's worth 50p aff their album!" Logie said.

"An' it's the only coupon movin' in here the night!" Wheech laughed, looking round at the amount of people who'd usually be nodding their heads in time to the music, but weren't.

The band reached a pause in their song and the leader desperately tried to get the crowd involved by clapping his hands above his head. It worked, and gave him a boost of confidence – until he realised people were shouting "Aff!" in time with their claps.

"There they go!" Wheech bellowed, joining the pointing and laughing as the guys on stage gave it up and wandered towards the safety of the backstage area. "Any more o' they coupons? They wurny that bad. Might get an album."

He emptied his last tin, and with no need to hide it, there was no need to hide in the stalls. "Let's go doon the front," he said. "Get ready for the mighty fuckin' Night Gerden."

The front four rows of seats had long gone. There was no point in them being there since, once seated, it was impossible to see anything on the stage. But the space seemed a bit bigger in the half-light as roadies moved gear on and off the platform. "That's AC/DC fur ye," Wheech said. "There's three mair rows away efter last night."

He turned round to catch up with one of those members of the Glasgow choir who were only ever seen in the venue, and whose names were never asked and never told, who spoke only in terms of what shows they'd seen, what shows they were going to see and what shows they'd like to see. Even as the threat of closure became ever more real, no one wanted it to spoil the fun – especially if it was the last of it.

Logie stared up at the stage. It didn't look like much: just wooden boards, painted black, generating nothing but the unpleasant sound of thumping roadies' feet, as if the guy in the flat upstairs had forgotten to take his work boots off, and so had all his mates. But that wasn't what the stage meant,

any more than Ally MacLeod would just be holding up a wee metal statue.

It almost made a grown man cry (and take the slagging for it) to think about the moments that had taken place up there. Patches on jackets and badges on lapels in every direction displayed the list. The Kinks, Neil Young, the Faces (out their nuts), Elton John, Slade, Mud, the Quo, Skynyrd, Uriah Heep, Argent, Wishbone Ash, Genesis. Marc Bolan (RIP), the

Rolling Fucking Stones, Mott The Hoople and Queen on the same night. And homegrown talent like Nazareth, Alex Harvey and, aye, Billy Connolly. Fuck sake – you couldn't take it in.

And Logie had been there. The Glasgow choir had all been there. Thousands of people in this outpouring of love and belief in music, that reduced the people who made it to tears, and made them dig deeper to work harder, and every single person in the room went away better for it. Nearly every night. For five years.

And now it was finishing. And that meant Logie would never be one of them, up there, giving till it hurt, giving till it meant more than anything ever had, giving until that balcony bounced like it was launching actual Apollo rockets at the moon.

It was too much to let go. What else was there? Living in Govan, going to work, having a few pints, watching the fitba', playing the Burns Howff every other weekend with your old mates, while everyone just kept getting older?

It wasn't enough. He'd seen too much. He couldn't let it go. It was bad enough for the four thousand people around him right now, but it was worse for him. Because he knew he had a right to be up there – and he wasn't going to make it, because up there would be gone in a matter of weeks.

Of course there were other stages, other venues. But they weren't the Apollo, and nothing ever could be, because the magic actually happened in the space between the musicians and the punters: in the air above the stalls, the canyon between the stage and the balcony, and the gaps between every individual member of the audience. That atmosphere only existed *here*.

The lights went down. The roar went up. The thunder of fans pelting into the frontstage area momentarily drowned out the count of four as the bouncers fixed their glares and Logie felt arms thrown round him. "Here we fuckin' go!" cried someone he'd never met as Night Garden began to play.

"You're Logie McFarlane!" grinned the guy who'd just grabbed him. "Fox Ache – brilliant! Nearly as good as them, know?" He had no choice but to move back and forth with the crowd around him. Everyone knew the words as the blues-based rock galloped towards the chorus. "*You're! Gonna! Be! Mine!*" the guy shouted tunelessly, but in time, throwing a pointed finger at the multi-coloured stage with each word.

Bobby Rycott beamed as bright as a spotlight, pointing back at faces he recognised (or pretended to) as he led them through the song. "*Ain't nothin' to it! Ain't nothin' you can do about it! You're gonna be mine!*" He turned away as a new cheer went up to welcome Dave Mitchell, who stepped up to the front and burst into his first guitar solo of the night.

"Mon then, Davie!" the fan bellowed, then turned and said: "Imagine bein' in a band wi' that boy, eh? *Eh!*" Then he finally let Logie go so to concentrate on playing air-guitar, bouncing like the balcony, as a nearby bouncer wished he could reach him to give him a slap.

Night Garden weren't going to struggle to keep the room on their side – or at least, that's how it seemed. It was well-known from their recent live album that they went from *You're Gonna Be Mine* straight into *Roll Easy* without a break, but the Glasgow choir refused to let it happen, roaring for a good thirty seconds until the band managed to get on with their next track.

But the euphoria didn't last. Logie had already seen there was something different about the chemistry between Rycott and Mitchell – in the past they'd stood at the front together, arm in arm, but tonight they were taking turns going upstage and downstage. And after *Roll Easy*, it felt as if the singer had deliberately waited until some of the energy had faded before speaking to the audience. "Good evening, Glasgow!" he said, failing to hide something less than positive in his voice.

"It's always nice to start a tour here," he went on after the next cheer had died down. "Well, it always has been in the past. You know why I like Glasgow?"

"The burds!" someone shouted.

"The Sellick!" shouted another.

Rycott smiled. "It's because, as soon as we cross the border, even our own crew start calling us 'Night Gerden'." His attempt at a Glaswegian accent got him a laugh. "No, the real reason is that you're honest with us," he want on, receiving more vocal approval. "You tell us what you think, and that's important. So it'll be... interesting... to hear what you think of this next one. This is our new single, out next week. it's called *Jump*." He paused, then added quietly: "Let's get it over with."

Mitchell could be seen glaring across the stage, just for a moment, before kicking off a powerful guitar riff. But while it was powerful, it was, for want of a better description, not a Night Garden riff. And as the bass and drums joined in, the truth was revealed. *It was a punk song.*

Most people didn't care at first. As far as they were concerned there was four-on-the-floor and that was all they needed to get their coupons moving. It wasn't until Rycott began to sing that it became obvious something was badly wrong.

He had a great voice. It was said he'd been tried out by Led Zeppelin, Free and several others at the end of the 60s, before they settled on Robert Plant and Paul Rodgers respectively. What he didn't have was a voice that could convincingly pull off the punk sneer that seemed to be required for the song. And worse, it was obvious that he didn't really want to try. "*Jump! Jump! Get movin'! Get it up and out!*" he sort-of sang and sort-of spoke.

"Get *whit*?" someone shouted nearby.

"Get ti' fuck!" someone else said.

By the time the song was finished – without a trademark Mitchell solo – the sense of unity in the room was long gone. Most of the audience still applauded, but it was far more polite and respectful than the animal roar that welcomed the earlier numbers.

A curious tense silence fell as eight thousand eyes looked to Rycott for an explanation. He couldn't offer it. He turned to stare at Mitchell, who wouldn't return his gaze, then told the audience: "Well, that's our new sound. Apparently." That earned him definite boos from various parts of the auditorium. "But, hey – you remember *Downward Spiral*?" The response was hopeful. "Well, here's *Downward Spiral*... the new version." The snarl of suspicion was more felt than heard,

but it was there.

Logie couldn't believe it as the song began. There were the chords. There was the trademark wee guitar lick. It was all there – but it was all different. Although, despite what a lot of people in the room thought, it wasn't all bad.

Once the band kicked in, he felt it instantly. A good song, played well, even if played more simply than it had been done in the past. Logie had to accept it: *it worked.* That was, until Rycott began singing. "*Feels like I've been here too long, can't do right for doing wrong…*" It wasn't that the vocal melody didn't lend itself to the faster, sharper, more empty vibe – it was that he just didn't seem to want to make it work.

Logie could tell all of that. But a lot of people around him couldn't. They weren't singers so it wasn't their job to know. All *they* knew was that a band who they'd trusted had confused them, and now seemed to be betraying them.

And that's when the fight started.

The guy who'd had his arm round Logie was happily pogoing around, regardless of how some people felt. He went to put his arm round someone else, but picked a guy who was standing in near-shock at what he was hearing. He took the move badly and pushed back – and within seconds six people, then twelve, then twenty, were involved in a front-and-centre barney.

That was a cue for those further up the stalls who felt equally bemused and confused. Violence was a good outlet, and the invitation had been extended. On the raised platform below the stage, the row of bouncers waited, calculating, until their colleagues from the back of the room were just about to arrive, then waded in with all limbs in motion, throwing the guilty and innocent in every direction, setting off new fights as they went, like they were firing 5p rockets from their sleeves.

Night Garden were coming across as many things, but they were at least professional. Or at least, most of them were. They kept playing, kept churning on through a song that, in all honestly, had something to say for itself in its punk form. But Rycott delivered one last, prophetic line: *"Been so tired living under a setting sun, I know, I know it's time to cut and run!"* Then he dropped his microphone and marched offstage, making a point of elbowing Mitchell as he passed.

Those who were still watching the stage erupted in fury, and the sound seemed to pull more violence out of those who'd started fighting. But Logie kept watching as Mitchell, his face betraying nothing but sheer determination, powered on through the song, only once signalling to his bandmates that they should keep going too.

"Logie! Get up there!" Wheech appeared at his side. "This

is your song, man! Sing it fur 'em! *Mon!*" He pulled his dazed friend towards the platform, as, from another direction, the Fox Ache fan appeared alongside. "Let's get him up there!" Wheech told him, and he agreed.

Still not quite certain of what was going on, Logie found himself with his hands against the front of the stage, while his companions leaned over to give him a punty up. A couple of bouncers saw what they were planning and began to rush towards them. But by that time Logie's hands were grasping the floor of the stage, and with another couple of shunts he had his elbows secure, even as the bouncers knocked Wheech and the fan to the ground beneath him.

But that was happening in another world. Logie stood with his back to the crowd, in some kind of limbo where, even though three members of Night Garden played on within feet of him, they and he were divided by miles.

It seemed like silence had fallen. After what felt like an age, he realised the shadows at the corners of his vision were roadies, coming to throw him from where he'd come. Then he realised the microphone was at his feet.

It was just like the Howff, really. He knew the song inside out. He believed the audience would dig what he did. He had a story to tell, and a crowd to listen, and a band to focus for him. That's all he needed. *That's all he'd ever needed.*

Logie grabbed the mic and spun round. The canyon opened before him – a deep, dark chasm with an invisible floor, because of the stage lights that blinded him from above. On the other side he could make out vague figures moving on the

balcony. It was *exactly* like the Howff. You couldn't make anything out. All there was to do was...

"Fucking sing, mate!" Mitchell shouted from behind.

"Feels like I've been here too long!" Logie sang. It wasn't his usual voice – it was something different. Something conjured up by this stage, this audience, this song, and the underlying fury at those who were trying to take it all away.

"Brilliant, mate! Keep going!" Mitchell said, signalling to his crew to leave the stage invader alone.

"Can't do right for doing wrong!" He turned the last word up, unlike the original, and it really added to the feeling. The news had spread through the stalls that something was going on, and the fighters had stopped fighting to find out what.

"If you want me to feel this bad, you're not the friend I thought I had!" The bouncers had clocked too, and an angry rabble of them scratched at the air below the stage.

The song went on and the Glasgow choir went with it, singing along, clapping along, but with Logie McFarlane clearly in charge. Mitchell appeared beside him, belting out the chords then throwing his arm around him, grinning and pointing, celebrating the moment.

"Been so tired living under a setting sun, I know, I know it's time to cut and run! Time to cut, cut, cut and run!" Mitchell led his bandmates into a final crescendo, holding the last chord open so it became part of the Apollo roar.

That's when Malky grabbed Logie from behind and dragged him off the stage.

It didn't matter how many people booed, or that the band and crew tried to rescue him. The bouncer was red with fury at being insulted on his own premises. It was personal. And it was going to hurt.

The backstage area led to a maze of badly-lit corridors, and Logie was battered against every door by Malky and three of his men, who all managed to get the odd kick and punch in as they went. "Smartarsed stuck-up bastard!" the leader snarled. "Think ye'r fuckin' somethin' but ye'r no! Ye'r just a" – *punch* – "wee" – *punch* – "fuckin'" – *punch* – "prick!"

He heard the sound of others, maybe Wheech, trying to rescue him, and being violently forced back for their efforts. He felt the fists and feet and heard the constant drone of insults. But it seemed to be happening to someone else, because he'd just sung his favourite song, with his favourite band, in the only venue that ever really mattered.

The fire door was kicked open and the bouncers took three long swings before heaving him into a pile of bin bags in the lane. Logie landed with a sickening thud, but it was just another part of the moment he'd been stuck in for the past minutes, and it didn't hurt. Although it probably would in the morning.

The door slammed.

Then it opened again.

Logie lay still, not looking for any further interaction with the security staff. Nevertheless, he found himself picked up by his collar and forced to sit nearly upright on weak, nearly-useless legs.

"You sang wi' Night Gerden," Malky said in a voice he'd never used to anyone but Apollo headliners before. "*You... fuckin' sang...* wi' fucking *Night Gerden.*"

"I fuckin' did an' all," Logie replied in a distant tone, looking the bouncer straight in the eye.

There was a flash of movement in the twilight, and a seven-inch single appeared in front of his face, followed a moment later with a marker pen. "Sign this."

Logie took the pen and added his autograph to the copy of *Jump C/W Downward Spiral (New Version).*

"Right. See ye later," Malky said, recovering his record and pen, and slamming the fire door behind him.

Logie collapsed back into the bin bags, then laughed his head off.

ALSO BY MARTIN KIELTY

APOLLO MEMORIES

The story of the legendary Glasgow venue where, from 1973 to 1985, they all played and they all came back. Added to the Rock And Roll Hall of Fame Permanent Collection, Scottish New Music Awards finalist, Daily Record Book of the Year, Daily Mail Critics' Choice, WH Smith Scottish Book of the Year shortlister.

SAHB STORY: THE TALE OF THE SENSATIONAL ALEX HARVEY BAND

The definitive biography, authorised by surviving members Zal Cleminson, Chris Glen, Hugh McKenna and Ted McKenna. Foreword by Joe Elliott of Def Leppard.

ALEX HARVEY: LAST OF THE TEENAGE IDOLS

Elegant harback photobook, featuring the work of award-winning photographer Janet Macoska. Added to the Rock And Roll Hall Of Fame Permanent Collection.

BIG NOISE: THE SOUND OF SCOTLAND

A journey down the side roads of Scottish popular music history.
Also available in cut-down edition *Big Noise From A Wee Country*.

ARE YE DANCIN'?

The first-ever inside story of how Scotland's ballrooms and dance halls remained a central part of Scottish culture throughout the 20th Century. With Eddie Tobin.

BILLY RANKIN'S SCHOOL OF ROCK

Notes for students of rock'n'roll from radio presenter and former Nazareth guitarist Billy Rankin. Foreword by Scottish rock icon Tom Russell.

SIMON THE FOX

A novel blending historical fiction with action, adventure and murder-mystery, based on the real-life Simon Fraser, notorious Jacobite, who was executed in 1747.

OLD THE FRONT PAGE

2000 years of headlines – Scottish history like you've never seen it before, the way a newspaper might have covered it. Foreword by acclaimed novelist Robert Low.

WWW.MARTINKIELTY.COM

Printed in Great Britain
by Amazon